TINYRANNOSAURUS
AND THE
BIGFOOTOSAURUS!

By
Nick Ward

meadowside
CHILDREN'S BOOKS

It was cold and snowy, but **Tinyrannosaurus (wrecks)** didn't mind.

He was the **roughest, toughest, fiercest** little dinosaur ever.
(He was wearing his warm hat and scarf too!)

He had been tobogganing with his friends all morning,
and now they were quite worn out.

"I know," said Tiny. "Let's build a snowman."

So Tinyrannosaurus and his friends built the **biggest** and **meanest** looking snowman you have ever seen, right on top of a tall hill.

"It looks just like a Bigfootosaurus," laughed Tiny.

Tiny and his friends danced around the snowman singing, "We're not afraid of the Bigfootosaurus."

Meanwhile . . .

on the other side of the hill, a **REAL**
Bigfootosaurus was wondering just who
was standing on the top of his hill.
(It looked like another Bigfoot and he
wasn't having that!)

"My hill," he grunted,
and started to march to the top.

"Silly old Bigfootosaurus!"
cried Tiny's friends, busy pulling faces at their snowman.

"My hill!" Bigfootosaurus grunted again, and with one swipe of his mighty paw, he squashed the snowman flat!

And, oh dear, Tiny and his friends were so busy laughing that they didn't notice their snowman had changed.

"A Bigfootosaurus couldn't scare me,"
said Dinoceros.
"If I met a real Bigfootosaurus,
I would throw snowballs at him,
Like this!"
The Bigfootosaurus grumbled.

"And if I met a real Bigfootosaurus,
I would pull his tail,
Like this!"
cried Baby Kong.
    The Bigfootosaurus growled.

"If I met a real Bigfootosaurus, I would scare him to pieces with my terrific **roar!**" bellowed Tiny.

"Grrrnash!"

Tiny's friends laughed.

Grrrnash!

The Bigfootosaurus raised his hairy arms and flexed his sharp claws...

"Oh yeah?" he bellowed.

He raced after them, his big monster feet
making the ground rumble and shake!

"Help, run!"
shrieked Tiny to his gang.
"OUR SNOWMAN HAS COME TO LIFE!"

Bigfootosaurus was
right behind them.

He lifted his big, hairy foot,
high above their heads.

"Rarrr!"
he roared...

. . . and brought his foot **crashing** down.

"Watch out!" cried Tiny.

But the big monster foot landed on Baby Kong's toboggan by mistake.

WOOSH!

He went skating past Tiny's friends at top speed. **"Help,"** he cried. "I can't stop!"

Good, thought Tiny. That will teach him a lesson.

The Bigfootosaurus was skating straight towards a deep and dangerous ravine.

"Help!"

he roared.
He was
really,
really
scared!

"Oh no, our poor snowman," cried Tinyrannosaurus as they watched him skate **closer** and **closer** to the edge of the ravine.

"What shall we do?"
Tiny and his friends chased after him, but he was going much too fast.

Then Tiny had a **brilliant** idea!

Tinyrannosaurus roared
his loudest roar.

"ROAR!"

It was so loud it shook
the snow right out of
a big fir tree.

It was so loud it shook
the snow right off
of the mountainside.

SPLAT!

The snow landed in a big heap on the ground.

PLOP!

Bigfootosaurus crashed into the big mound of snow and disappeared inside.

WOOSH!

Everything went very quiet.

"Are you all right, Snowman?"
asked Tinyrannosaurus, creeping nervously up to the pile of snow.

POP!

Bigfootosaurus stuck his head out of the top.

"Oh dear! That's **not** our snowman," cried Tiny.

"That's a **real** Bigfootosaurus. **EVERYBODY RUN!**"

"**STOP!**" bellowed the Bigfootosaurus, and everybody stopped. "You saved me. Thank you. That was some **MIGHTY** roar!"

Tinyrannosaurus was so pleased and so proud, he roared again.

A **terrific** roar!

An **earth shaking** roar!

"No, Tiny!"
cried his friends, but it was too late . . .

For Carl,
the Smellyfootosaurus!

N.W.

First published in 2007
by Meadowside Children's Books
185 Fleet Street, London, EC4A 2HS
www.meadowsidebooks.com

Text and illustrations © Nick Ward 2007
The right of Nick Ward to be identified as the author
and illustrator of this work has been asserted by him
in accordance with the Copyright, Designs and Patents Act, 1988

A CIP catalogue record for this book
is available from the British Library
Printed in Indonesia

10 9 8 7 6 5 4 3 2 1